If your child struggles with a word, you can encourage "sounding it out," but keep in mind that not all words can be sounded out. Your child might pick up clues about a word from the picture, other words in the sentence, or any rhyming patterns. If your child struggles with a word for more than five seconds, it is usually best to simply say the word.

Most of all, remember to praise your child's efforts and keep the reading fun. After you have finished the book, ask a few questions and discuss what you have read together. Rereading this book multiple times may also be helpful for your child.

Try to keep the tips above in mind as you read together, but don't worry about doing everything right. Simply sharing the enjoyment of reading together will increase your child's reading skills and help to start your child off on a lifetime of reading enjoyment!

Changing Places

A We Both Read Book

Level 1–2

Text Copyright © 2017 by D. J. Panec
Illustrations Copyright © 2017 by Andy Elkerton
All rights reserved

We Both Read® is a trademark of Treasure Bay, Inc.

Published by Treasure Bay, Inc.
P.O. Box 119
Novato, CA 94948 USA

Printed in Malaysia

Library of Congress Catalog Card Number: 2016940079

Hardcover ISBN: 978-1-60115-297-8
Paperback ISBN: 978-1-60115-298-5

Visit us online at:
www.webothread.com

PR-11-16

Changing Places

By D. J. Panec

Illustrated by Andy Elkerton

TREASURE BAY

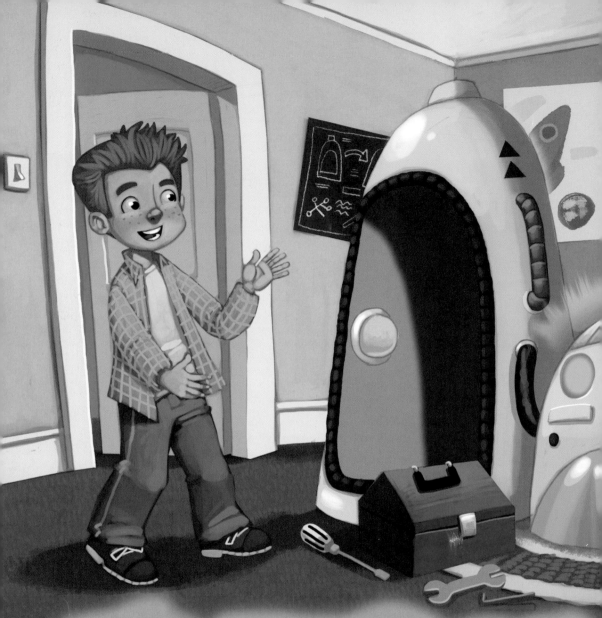

"Here it is! The most amazing invention ever!" I proudly threw a switch and my newest creation started to glow with energy. "I present to you—the Place Changer 5000!"

I waited for the cheers, but all I got was a blank stare from my sister, **Kayla**, and a wide yawn from her cat, Fluffy.

"You see," I explained, "I go in this booth and someone else goes in the other booth. Then I press the button and we **change places**!"

Kayla gave me a funny look.

"Why?" she asked.

"Why what?" I said.

"Why do you want to **change places**?"

3

"Because it's totally cool," I said. "The machine instantly transports you from one **booth** to the **other booth**."

Kayla crinkled her nose. "Mike, if you want to be in the **other booth,** why don't you just go there in the first place?"

I slapped my forehead in frustration. Clearly she needed a demonstration. So I called in my assistant, Rex.

"In you go, Rex," I said.

Rex jumped into one **booth**. I went into the **other** booth.

"Three, two, one! Go!" I yelled, and I pressed the button.

The machine started to rattle and shake with a wild zapping energy. Then suddenly it stopped and, as calmly as I could, I stepped out of the Place Changer. As predicted, I had transported **myself** to the other booth, changing places with Rex. I smiled proudly. "Well, Kayla?" I said. "What do you think now?"

Kayla looked more than amazed. She looked stunned.

"What do I think?" she said. "I think you are a dog."

I looked down at **myself** and yelped, "Fur! Paws! Oh, no!"

I looked at where Rex should have been, and I saw myself sitting there like a dog.

Our bodies hadn't changed places—only our brains! My brain was in Rex's body—and Rex's brain was in mine. I had to change us back **again**!

Unfortunately, Rex took off in my body. I raced after him and found him at his food **bowl** chowing down on dog food.

"Rex! Stop that!" I said. "That's disgusting and it's going in *my* stomach."

I grabbed the **bowl** away from Rex and set it up on the table.

Then Rex picked up his ball and took off running **again**.

"Rex, stop!" I yelled. "I have to change us back."

Just then, Kayla's cat, Fluffy, walked in.

"Hey, Mike! Look at me," she said.

"Oh, no!" I yelled. "What did you *do*? And where's Kayla?"

"I'm Kayla!" she said with a big smile.

"Yes, I get that, Kayla. So then where's Fluffy, who I assume is now running around in *your* body? And who said you could use my machine without asking?"

 "You didn't say I had to ask first," she said.

"We have to change you back," I said. "Now!"

"Aw, not yet," said Kayla. "I like being a kitty cat."

"Do you know what Mom is going to do if she sees us like this?" I asked.

Suddenly I heard barking in our **front yard**. "Oh, great!" I groaned. "Rex got out!" I turned to Kayla. "Fine. Be a cat. Just help me get Rex back inside."

Before we went out, I checked to see if anyone was on the street. I was especially worried about seeing a certain kid that lived down the block. I always did my best to avoid Billy, even when I didn't look like a dog.

The coast was clear. At **least** I thought it was.

Rex was in the **front yard**. He was digging up Mom's flowers. "Nooo!" I yelled. "Bad Rex! Bad doggie!"

Kayla shook her head. "Mom is going to be mad."

"Yes," I said, "but at **least** she'll be mad at Rex, not me."

Kayla shrugged. "Then you better not be in Rex's body when she finds out."

I grabbed Rex's shirt collar and pulled him toward the house. Just then, Fluffy ran into the yard and straight up a tree.

Of course, it didn't look like Fluffy. It looked just like Kayla, which was natural since Fluffy now had Kayla's body.

 "Fluffy!" yelled Kayla. "You come down right now! I do not like being in trees!"

Fluffy said, "Meow."

Just then, Kayla's friend from next door came over. She looked up into the tree. "What are you doing up there, Kayla?"

"That's not me, Kimmy," said Kayla. "That's Fluffy. I'm right here. And look! I'm a cat!"

Kimmy looked at Kayla and squealed. "A cat! Oh, I've always wanted to be a cat!"

"Mike can help you," said Kayla.

"What? No, I can't!" I said.

Kayla ignored me. "But you have to bring your own cat to go in Mike's Place Changer machine."

"No!" I said firmly. "You cannot be a cat, Kimmy."

I turned back to get Rex and saw that he was digging up more flowers.

Then Billy showed up.

Letting Billy see me as a dog would be the end of me. So I hid behind a tree.

Billy spotted Rex, who was covered in dirt from all his digging. "Hey, Mikey," he said. "You're getting pretty dirty there. Need some help?" Then he kicked some dirt on me. I mean on Rex.

This was only going to get worse.

I had to get Rex away from Billy, but what could I do?

Then, I saw Rex's ball under the tree.

I threw the ball and Rex jumped and ran after it.

Only Rex didn't run so well with my body. He just crawled really fast.

Billy laughed hysterically. "Mikey's crawling! Like a big baby!"

I needed a plan to get Billy to go away. Then it occurred to me. I could just pretend to be Rex!

"Stay here **behind** the tree," I hissed to Kayla the cat. "Stay there," I **growled** to Fluffy, who was still up in the tree.

I snuck up **behind** Billy and **growled,** "Grrrrrr!"

Billy jumped. "Rex! How did you get out here?"

I growled again. "Do you think walls can stop me?"

Billy stared at me like he was seeing a ghost. "Did . . . did you just talk?"

"Yes, and I'm talking to *you*, Billy," I said, showing my doggy teeth. "Now how about you go home and don't come **around** again until you've changed into a nice kid." Then I growled my scariest growl. "Or next time you're mean, I will come bite you—and have a talk with your parents."

Billy screamed and ran off. I think our little talk was a big success. Now I just had to find Rex. And Kayla. And Fluffy. And change us all back.

I turned **around** and there was Kimmy, holding her cat.

"Hi, Mike!" she said. "You know, I like you better as a dog."

I grabbed Rex, who was now barking at Kimmy's cat. "Kimmy," I said, "how very *not* nice to see you again. And no, I will not be turning you into a cat today."

"But Kayla gets to be a cat," Kimmy whined.

Kayla suddenly noticed Fluffy had come down and was licking Kimmy's cat. "Ewww! Stop that, Fluffy!" she **shouted**.

Rex was barking, Kayla was shouting, Kimmy was whining . . .

Then we **heard** a **voice** from the house.

"Mike! Kayla!"

Oh, no! It was Mom.

"We're out front!" **shouted** Kayla before I could
stop her.

"What are you doing out there?" I **heard** Mom's
voice getting closer.

"Quick, Kayla," I said, "pretend to be Fluffy!"

Kayla looked confused. "But I *am* Fluffy. Sort of . . ."

"No, I mean get down and act like a cat," I told her. "Just meow."

"We're playing cats and dogs, Mom!" I called into the house.

Mom stepped out of the front door. "I hope you are playing nice," she said.

"Meow!" said Fluffy.

"Meow!" said Kayla.

Mom looked around. "Where is Mike?" she asked.

Rex came crawl-running up to Mom. "Mike, it's nice to see you playing with your sister, but how did you get so dirty?"

"Ruff!" answered Rex.

"Hello, Mrs. Burk," said Kimmy.

"Hello, Kimmy," said Mom. "Are you going to be a cat too?"

"That was the plan," sighed Kimmy.

Suddenly Mom **pointed** and screamed, "My flower bed!"

Mom turned to Rex. She **pointed** to the dug up dirt and flowers. "Mike, did Rex dig up my flower bed?"

"Ruff!" said Rex.

"Mrs. Burk!" said Kimmy.

 Mom looked at Rex. "Mike, I expect an answer."

Of course, Rex couldn't answer. And if I said anything Mom would probably **scream** and faint and take away the Place Changer 5000.

"Mrs. Burk!" said Kimmy again.

"What *is* it, Kimmy?"

"Kayla's a great kitty, but she is up pretty high and that branch could **break**."

Kimmy pointed up into the tree.

"KAYLA!" Mom **screamed**. "What are you doing up there?"

"Meow!" said Fluffy.

"You come down right now," said Mom, "before you fall and **break** your neck!"

Mom had her back to me, so I said, "Maybe you could get her down with a ladder."

"Good idea, Mike!" said Mom. Then she called up to Fluffy. "Kayla, stay right there!"

As soon as Mom disappeared into the house, I jumped up and turned to Kayla. "Can you get Fluffy out of the tree? We've got to get to the Place Changer 5000 and change bodies with Rex and Fluffy before Mom gets back."

"But I want more time being a kitty," said Kayla.

"And I want a turn being a kitty," said Kimmy.

"Look," I said, "if we don't change back, Mom will make me get rid of the Place Changer."

"So I could never be a kitty again?"

I shook my head. "Never."

Kayla called up to Fluffy. "Fluffy! I've got treats!" And just like that, Fluffy scampered down.

I grabbed Rex and turned to Kimmy. "Thanks for your help with my mom."

"You're welcome," she said grinning. "Just remember you owe me and Kayla a kitty-cat play date."

I got Kayla, Rex, and Fluffy into the house.

Then, we snuck down the hall and into my room.

"OK," I said, "Kayla and Fluffy, you go first."

I put Fluffy into one side. Kayla went into the other side.

"Hey, everyone! I'm home," a voice called out from down the hall.

It was Dad. I heard his footsteps moving toward us.

Time was running out! I had to work fast!

I pushed Rex into the booth with Fluffy. Then I jumped in with Kayla and pushed the button.

The Place Changer started humming!

The machine zapped wildly with electricity, then suddenly stopped. I heard Dad's footsteps moving away.

"Honey," I heard him saying, "what's the ladder for? Here, let me get that."

I quickly went over to the other booth and saw Rex and Fluffy step out. "Look," I shouted. "I did it! I changed them back!"

Kayla stepped out and said, "Maybe you changed them back, but now you look just like me!"

I looked down at myself. "Oh, no," I said. "I'm a girl! I'm you! OK. This is not good."

"Ewww!" screamed Kayla, looking at herself. "I'm a boy. This is so gross!"

"Meow!" said Rex.

"Woof!" said Fluffy.

"No need to panic," I said. "Quick! **Everyone** back in the machine!"

Everyone got in.

I pushed the button and said, "This time I'm sure it will work."

If you liked *Changing Places*, here is another We Both Read® book you are sure to enjoy!

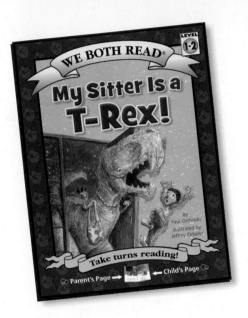

My Sitter Is a T-Rex!

Mom and Dad rush out the door as soon as the new babysitter arrives. But the new sitter is a T-Rex! In this fun-filled adventure, a boy deals with the scariest and funniest babysitter ever.